leapfrog

Jack's Party

First published in 2000
Franklin Watts
96 Leonard Street
London
EC2A 4XD

Franklin Watts Australia
45-51 Huntley Street
Alexandria
NSW 2015

A CIP catalogue record for this book is available
from the British Library.

ISBN 0 7496 3729 3 (hbk)
ISBN 0 7496 4389 7 (pbk)

Series Editor: Louise John
Series Advisor: Dr Barrie Wade
Series Designer: Jason Anscomb

Printed in China

For Amy Hodgeson – A.B

For Tom and Hannah – C.H

Jack's Party

by Ann Bryant

Illustrated by Claire Henley

W
FRANKLIN WATTS
LONDON•SYDNEY

It was Jack's birthday party and he was having a great time, until ...

Amy tripped over her shoe lace and Jack heard her mumble, "I hate painting faces!"

"Me too!" everyone agreed.

Jack went red.

Jack's mum came back
from the kitchen.

"Who wants to play pass the parcel?" she asked.

Jack bit his lip.

He knew what was

inside the parcel.

"I'm not joining in," he said.

The music started.
The parcel went round
the circle.

The music stopped.

Tom ripped off the first layer.

"Let's play musical statues,"
said Jack.

"Pass the parcel is for babies."

"No!" everyone shouted.

"We want pass the parcel!"

Jasmine ripped off another layer of paper.

Jack pressed the stop
button on the CD player.

"Oh no, it's broken! Let's watch a video," Jack said.

Jack's mum pressed the
play button again.

Molly ripped off the next
layer of paper.

Josh ripped off the one
after that.

Jack held his breath.

Everyone watched as Amy ripped off the last layer.

"Great, it's face paints!"
shouted Amy.

"I thought you said you hated painting faces," said Jack.

"No, I said I hate **tying laces**," said Amy.

"Painting faces is great!"

Leapfrog has been specially designed to fit the requirements of the National Literacy Strategy. It offers real books for beginning readers by top authors and illustrators.

There are 31 Leapfrog stories to choose from:

The Bossy Cockerel

Written by Margaret Nash, illustrated by Elisabeth Moseng

Bill's Baggy Trousers

Written by Susan Gates, illustrated by Anni Axworthy

Mr Spotty's Potty

Written by Hilary Robinson, illustrated by Peter Utton

Little Joe's Big Race

Written by Andy Blackford, illustrated by Tim Archbold

The Little Star

Written by Deborah Nash, illustrated by Richard Morgan

The Cheeky Monkey

Written by Anne Cassidy, illustrated by Lisa Smith

Selfish Sophie

Written by Damian Kelleher, illustrated by Georgie Birkett

Recycled!

Written by Jillian Powell, illustrated by Amanda Wood

Felix on the Move

Written by Maeve Friel, illustrated by Beccy Blake

Pippa and Poppa

Written by Anne Cassidy, illustrated by Philip Norman

Jack's Party

Written by Ann Bryant, illustrated by Claire Henley

The Best Snowman

Written by Margaret Nash, illustrated by Jörg Saupe

Eight Enormous Elephants

Written by Penny Dolan, illustrated by Leo Broadley

Mary and the Fairy

Written by Penny Dolan, illustrated by Deborah Allwright

The Crying Princess

Written by Anne Cassidy, illustrated by Colin Paine

Jasper and Jess

Written by Anne Cassidy, illustrated by François Hall

The Lazy Scarecrow

Written by Jillian Powell, illustrated by Jayne Coughlin

The Naughty Puppy

Written by Jillian Powell, illustrated by Summer Durantz

Freddie's Fears

Written by Hilary Robinson, illustrated by Ross Collins

Cinderella

Written by Barrie Wade, illustrated by Julie Monks

The Three Little Pigs

Written by Maggie Moore, illustrated by Rob Hefferan

Jack and the Beanstalk

Written by Maggie Moore, illustrated by Steve Cox

The Three Billy Goats Gruff

Written by Barrie Wade, illustrated by Nicola Evans

Goldilocks and the Three Bears

Written by Barrie Wade, illustrated by Kristina Stephenson

Little Red Riding Hood

Written by Maggie Moore, illustrated by Paula Knight

Rapunzel

Written by Hilary Robinson, illustrated by Martin Impey

Snow White

Written by Anne Cassidy, illustrated by Melanie Sharp

The Emperor's New Clothes

Written by Karen Wallace, illustrated by François Hall

The Pied Piper of Hamelin

Written by Anne Adeney, illustrated by Jan Lewis

Hansel and Gretel

Written by Penny Dolan, illustrated by Graham Philpot

The Sleeping Beauty

Written by Margaret Nash, illustrated by Barbara Vagnozzi